Carol Habrovitsky has lived in Glasgow for 50 years. She is married with 1 son and 3 grandchildren. Born in London, she trained as nurse in the Royal Free Hospital in London. She has worked as a nurse in Glasgow in hospitals, industry, public health, neurology, casualty eventually running a large nursing home as matron. Nursing has been her lifelong love where she learnt so much more about life as well as nursing. In retirement, she has written poetry and volunteered in health inspections of hospitals. Her hobbies include Tai Chi, travelling, language studies and spending time with her family.

Best Wishes

Carol   2020

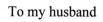

To my husband

Carol Habrovitsky

No Highway

AUSTIN MACAULEY PUBLISHERS™

LONDON • CAMBRIDGE • NEW YORK • SHARJAH

A CIP catalogue record for this title is available from the British Library.

ISBN 9781528994088 (Paperback)
ISBN 9781528994095 (ePub e-book)

www.austinmacauley.com

First Published (2020)
Austin Macauley Publishers Ltd
25 Canada Square
Canary Wharf
London
E14 5LQ

Husband, son, neighbour & friends

Chapter 1

On a bright sunlit day, all seemed serene as Joan prepared for the onslaught of human bodies which would shortly come flying through the doors of the casualty department. This was the start of the annual Glasgow holiday and with the good weather the roads would be crowded with cars driven by people who only drove on their way, on their usual way to Blackpool for the Glasgow Fair.

But these people were not to become the problem that was to face Joan this 'Fair' weekend. As a senior member of the nursing in casualty, Joan had seen many Glasgow Fair's Fridays pass, both good and bad. The weather, not really affecting the mad dash by all out of Glasgow. However, this one, Joan would remember for a long time.

Joan was aroused from her day-dreaming by the sudden siren of an ambulance. She quickly checked all the equipment in the resuscitation room and walked calmly out towards the main hall of casualty. As she approached, she saw two heavy built ambulance men carrying a long flat body on a stretcher. Joan, tall herself at 5'8" saw that the body was a very tall young man. By the speed ambulance men moved, Joan knew they were making for the room she had just left. She turned back and awaited them. All her senses were geared towards the emergency. The excitement, tension, concentration were reflected in her sparkling eyes and erect figure. Within minutes the stretcher was placed on the couch and a tall blond doctor was coming to the top end of the stretcher where Joan stood. Joan looked down and saw a mess of curly hair covered in blood, a white face and one arm at a right angle to the couch. The body was still, and the breathing shallow but regular, the pupils reacting sluggishly to Joan's bright torch light. She took the pulse which was rapid and irregular, the blood pressure was falling. These signs and symptoms she reported to the doctor. This man was bleeding somewhere and was going into shock. Immediate treatment was required. The ambulance men had done well in rushing in this man. Joan turned to the doctor and calmly stated her findings. He was already looking for the bleeding point. It was a deep laceration with glass in it, behind the left ear. As well as a fracture of the right arm. But why was he unconscious. The doctor asked Joan to get further details from the ambulance men. She quickly slipped outside to the tea room where she knew the ambulance men would have gone for a quick cup of tea before continuing on their busy duties. In the meantime, the doctor stitched up the laceration behind the ear. Re-examined the young man or further injuries. Wrote out a card for X-ray of the arm. By this time, the inert body was beginning to groan and moan. When Joan returned, the look of relief on the doctor's face told her that the injuries were not serious. She had not been able to get much information. All the ambulance men were that they had found the young man lying unconscious by a telephone box surrounded by glass. A passer-by had called them but could not identify him or give any further information.

Joan began to undress the young man. He was wearing blue denim, rather dirty, a blue shirt and a bright red tie, almost the same colour as the blood in his hair. In his pockets she only found an address book, rather well used, an empty wallet, hose keys and some change. No identification of any sort. Joan turned to the doctor, who read her thoughts, told her to arrange admission to the surgical ward at least until they could ascertain who the young man was. The young man was becoming restless and his eyes, on opening were roaming the room not fixing on one place. Joan bent over him and said quietly to him, "Who are you? Does it hurt anywhere?"

He seemed to understand and pushed his injured arm up to his head, but did not actually speak.

By now, the porters had arrived and Joan wrote out all the details she had, listing the clothes, putting the money and keys in an envelope and handed them over to the porters to transport the young man on to the ward trolley and left casualty.

It was now time for Joan's lunch, another nurse appeared at the door to relieve her. Joan thanked her and walked purposefully towards the canteen. She wondered as she went, *How many bodies would arrive on this fateful day.* Joan was not very hungry. She ate a small salad and decided to follow up this last case. So she went up to the surgical ward. The sister on duty was a friend of hers and by now might have more details on the young man. Joan thought to herself what a good-looking man he was.

On the surgical ward, it was busy. They had been receiving patients all day and there had been many operations. Now visitors were flocking in and the nurses' changeover was in progress. Joan approached a sister and quickly started her business. She was directed to the bed close to the nurses' station, where the young man restlessly lay, kicking at the cot sides and pushing of the blankets and sheets. His eyes opened on her approach, and he turned painfully his head towards her. She said quietly as she drew up a chair, "Who are you?"

The young man smiled and answered monosyllable, "Michael." As Joan was about to ask more questions, a nurse came up to her.

"Sorry to interrupt you," she said. "But casualty are screaming for help."

Joan rose and briefly mumbled, "She would be back." She rushed off to casualty

In casualty, two men were in the main hall shouting at the top of their voices at each other. A woman was doubled over a chair, and Joan could see the blonde doctor in her room. In she went and saw his sigh of relief. He was pleased to see her as the other nurse had gone to attend a mother and child in another room, and he had a large obese man on the couch who had obviously taken an overdose and was drunk. The doctor was trying to put a tube down the shouting, abusive, violent man to pump out his stomach. Joan held the arms and legs, which took a lot of her strength. However, she was used to doing this. It happened frequently in casualty. With the patient restrained, the doctor quickly got the tube down, and the stomach mess was pumped out. The man stopped struggling. And the doctor signalled for Joan to take over, as he moved out towards the other room.

Joan was kept busy for the rest of her shift and did not think of 'Michael' until she was preparing to leave. She decided she was curious and would go up to see him again upstairs. She wondered what had really happened to him. When she entered the ward, she saw Michael lying peacefully with an elderly woman by his side. She went into the office and asked the nurse on duty if they got more information on Michael. All they knew was that the elderly lady was his mother, and they lived a little distance from the telephone box where he had been found. When they asked Michael for his next of kin, he had given the address from which the police brought this elderly woman in. Joan was curiously attracted to this young man. Michael saw her, raised his eyes and the plea in them decided for her. Joan walked over and breezily said, "How are you, Michael?" He responded and introduced his mother.

They made polite conversation and then his mother turned to Joan and said, "Will you stay with him for a while as I must get back home before it is dark?"

"Certainly," said Joan. Michael's mother left. Joan turned back to Michael and waited patiently for him to speak; part of all nurses' job. Michael watched and many thoughts rushed through his mind. *Should he tell her his secrets and seek her help? No, not after what had happened on the phone. He had better not involve her.* So, he just smiled at Joan. Joan decided to begin the conversation. She told him about herself. Including a few questions. Michael only gave the minimum answers and then seemed to drop off to sleep. After a while, Joan was sure he was fast asleep, she rose and made her way off the ward and to her own room in the nurses' home. She was very tired.

The nurses' home was quiet and Joan had a nice hot bath before snuggling down into a warm bed. Her thoughts were

Michael as well as all the other events of this Fair Friday. She drifted off to sleep and awoke refreshed and ready for a new day. Joan decided she would solve the problem by visiting Michael before she went on duty.

When she arrived at the surgical ward, she saw Michael lying still staring into space. She walked over towards his bed and asked, "How are you today?"

He remained silent. Joan wondered what she should do. Suddenly Michael turned to her with the same smile as his mother's, asked her, "Who are you, and have you come to help me?" Joan explained she had been the first to see him in casualty and had visited him last night with his mother. She also said that if he told her his problem she would try to help. Michael hesitantly told her how he had been trying to stop being the middleman in a drug ring, as he had been offered his first job which included a house in a new neighbourhood. It was suitable for both him and his mother, but his mother did not know about his involvement in drugs and he wanted to get out before he started his new job. He had gone to phone the leader of the drug gang, who had warned him of serious consequences if he withdrew. The leader had threatened him that if he left them, he would never see his new job or house. So, when he left the telephone box, something hard had hit him and someone had pulled sharply on his arm as he fell to the ground. Now he was frightened of leaving the hospital, and what the drug ring would do to him. Perhaps they would even get at his poor mother. He was so worried, he told Joan as he pleadingly looked up at her.

Joan was stunned. What could she do? There was no reason for him to stay in hospital. His arm would heal and his head injury was superficial. She wondered about the police. She turned to Michael and asked him if he wanted her to get in touch with the Police for him? The look of relief was a true 'thank you' for Joan. Michael was now exhausted and lay quietly with his eyes closed. As Joan rose to leave, a heavy-set policeman came towards her.

"Is this Michael Stone?" he asked.

"Yes," she said. Perhaps this was her chance. However, the policeman continued, "Is he fit to answer my questions?"

Joan replied in the affirmative and told the policeman, Michael had some questions for him too. So, she sadly left the policeman and Michael in deep conversation and went on duty in casualty for another interesting day

Chapter 2

Joan was busy all the rest of her shift and on her way home she wondered what had happened to Michael. She would pop up to the ward on her way to work tomorrow. Joan lived in the nurses' home with all the other staff nurses and some student and pupil nurses. As her parents had promised to help her, she was saving hard to afford her own place. As a staff nurse, she was reasonably well paid but flats were expensive and hard to find near the hospital. Perhaps one day, she would get a sister's post, preferably in casualty. This was her first choice of ward placement, and she had always enjoyed the unexpectedness of the work there. The immediate response needed there stimulated her. Also, the junior doctors treated the nurses nicer and did not look down on the staff as some did in the wards. There was a senior consultant but they rarely saw him.

Joan had enjoyed her 'Hands on training'. No university for her. During her training, she mixed both with other types of nurses such as pupil nurses, student physiotherapists, student speech therapists. The pupil nurses did a two-year course to make them state-enrolled nurses. This type of nursing was set up in the Second World War to replace trained staff who were working in the field of war. Some of these nurses were excellent but very territorial. Not liking young student nurses on their wards. Other enrolled nurses went into geriatrics or children's homes.

Joan did her three years general training, working in all branches of care from medical wards to surgical wards, operating theatres as well as children's wards and psychiatric units. These she did not especially like, as in psychiatrics, there were fully trained, mostly male nurses who looked down on student nurses and gave them the lowest jobs to do. Also, some of the procedures frightened Joan with their intensity. Joan did not want to leave Glasgow to gain further experience, so she decided she would apply for a staff nurse's place in casualty which she really liked. Joan enjoyed her work and found that Monday was the busiest day. So, she had no time to think of Michael. On her way off duty, she went up to the ward and found Michael's bed empty. She asked sister where he had gone. She said home. Because Joan worked the Fair weekend, she was due the next weekend off, and planned to go down to Arran where her parents had a holiday home. This had been the family's holiday every year. The house was in Lamlash a beautiful village overlooking Holy Island. This was a lovely island for children's adventure but was now curtailed due to the 'Buddhist retreat' there. However, Lamlash never changed. So, on Saturday morning, Joan set off to Arran.

Her father picked her up from the ferry and Joan started to relax. Four glorious days off in good sunshine with good food and her parents. The crossing from Ardrossan to Brodick was busy as it was a holiday time. Many people jumped on the local bus that did a tour of the whole island stopping anywhere either to pick people up, drop shopping or have a chat. Life in Arran is slower than on the mainland. Joan's dad drove slowly up the hill and over passed the busy golf course and down to the main road of Lamlash turning into a small lane to their cottage with roses around the door. It had a living room, a fitted kitchen; which her dad had put in, as well as two bedrooms upstairs with a new bathroom. Joan kissed her waiting mum and ran up the stairs to see the new bathroom and change. The bathroom was bathed in sunshine and had a bath, shower and toilet all in pure white. Dad had done it all by himself as he was really a retired plumber from Stephens (The Glasgow shipbuilders).

Lamlash was quiet, and Joan enjoyed it. As she came down the stairs, she decided to wander to the post office shop to hear the latest gossip. She heard her friend Ruth had had a baby boy so she brought a little rattle and wandered off to see

Ruth. Her mother had reminded her to be back for tea at 5 p.m. Ruth lived just off the road to Whiting Bay with her husband (an oil rig worker) and now their baby. Ruth was delighted to see Joan and showed off baby Jamie who was six months and teething. So the two girls chattered away and decided to put the baby into the pram and go for a walk. Gossiping along the road, Ruth told Joan that Richard had returned from his year-long wanderings as she had met him in the post office. Joan once fancy him but when he went off on his wanderings she forgot him. Whilst they talked, the baby Jamie fell asleep and they reached the crossroads with the main Lamlash Road. They heard an almighty scream and crunch of wheels. A lorry was perched on the edge of the sea and everyone had run out of the post office. Two people had come out of the hotel next door to get in their car, and been hit too. Ruth gave the baby to the postmistress and ran with Joan to the scene.

Police and a fire engine appeared along with an ambulance from the nearby Arran Memorable Hospital.

The police cleared the road, the fire engineers got the unconscious driver out of the lorry, and Joan and Ruth went to attend the couple lying on the road. The lady was crying, "Help me, my legs." The man seemed dazed and semi-conscious. The ambulance returned to get the couple, and Joan and Ruth walked along to the hospital at the end of the Road. Ruth asked the postmistress to get her mother to take the baby. When Ruth and Joan reached the hospital, they knew they would have to help. Bang, went Joan's holiday. This hospital was always short of staff, especially in the summer. So, when they got there, they were told the lorry driver was being airlifted to Inverclyde hospital, the two elderly people were in the receiving area, and Joan and Ruth went to sister's office to find out the extent of their injuries. Sister had asked for a local doctor to see them as the doctor on duty had gone with the helicopter to Inverclyde with a staff nurse. The GP was with the lady, and the man was being cleaned up by the staff on duty. Sister asked Joan and Ruth if they could possibly come in tomorrow as she would be particularly short-staffed then. They both agreed but Ruth had to ask her mother to take Jamie, and Ruth was officially on maternity leave. Joan was not keen as she had only four days off but would at least come in, in the morning.

Ruth was also a trained nurse having trained with Joan at the Royal Infirmary in Glasgow but married Alan on qualifying from Arran and working as a health visitor in Lamlash attached to the local GP Ruth was, thus, known locally and very popular. Her parents had retired to Arran and were friendly with Joan's parents. Ruth often helped out at the Arran Memorial Hospital especially in the summer months when Alan was at sea. However, just now Ruth was off on maternity leave having just had baby, Jamie. So, she had to ask her mother to help out the next day. Joan was prepared to give up her Sunday, day off, to help too. Thus, making it a busman's holiday for her. They both arrived at the hospital, as the night shift were leaving. The elderly lady had been admitted to a ward, and the husband had been cleaned up and returned to the hotel. So, Ruth went off to see the man. A Mr Peabody and Joan went up to the ward.

Mrs Peabody was lying restless flat on her back with one arm in a sling and two legs strung up on a pulley. As the ward was busy with other sick holiday patients, sister asked Joan to attend to Mrs Peabody. When she approached Mrs Peabody, she was waving her good arm around. Joan sat down next to her and started to speak to her.

Chapter 3

Michael recovered from his stay in hospital returning both home and to work. His mother was eagerly awaiting news of their impending move. She was busy cleaning out and Michael had to restrict her from his room. He was an 'Ardent Rangers' supporter with posters of his favourite players on his walls. The new season would start soon, and Michael had a season ticket which he was very proud of having brought it when he had served his time as an apprentice plumber. He now was (a plumber's liner off) already a journeyman. That is a time served apprentice of over five years and now promoted to a liner off. This entitled him to go on to the ship and line off routes of various piping systems, in the double bottoms of the ship, from plans received from the ships drawing office.

Some of the plans were diagrammatic systems showing the potential routes which he had to mark on the ship and draw out individual pipe sketches which would be sent to the plumber's shop for manufacture and later installed on the ship. Later on, when the accommodation was being structured a general arrangement drawing would come from the drawing office indicating routes of pipes, electrician's trays and ventilation systems etc. The liner off from each discipline would fight their corner for the best route for their individual department. It would lend itself for various arguments. In other words, who got in first, won. Michael's boss was 'Big Jimmie', a large older man with an over excitable nature especially after a weekend gambling. Michael was a pleasant calm man and often did homer's work (for outsiders) at the weekends in people's own homes. His father had been a time served cabinet maker and had died a few years ago. However, he taught Michael the work ethic. A fair day's work for a fair day's pay and punctuality came from his mother. She was a cleaner in hospital for many years; now retired. Every morning Michael got the yellow tram from the Gorbals to the shipyard in time to clock on. His pieces were carried in a bag to work, made up by his mother every night. She would watch him going out and coming home each day. Many of Michael's friends were like him – Rangers supporters – and they would meet up locally before the games and afterwards to discuss the events in local pubs. Although Michael was not a real drinker, he did not like Wednesday games as it meant: everyone came in next day in a foul mood if their team lost. Also, it was harder to get up in the morning after a game. However, Saturdays were different. Michael liked to go over to the 'Barrows' and wander around, sometimes buying Rangers' souvenirs or records as he loved music of any sort and had quite a big collection, which he had told his mother that wherever they went the records would go with them.

Chapter 4

Joan went over to Michael, touched his hand and whispered, "Keep going," before leaving to go on duty in casualty. She would be on duty for the next few days and then be off to go to see 'Evita' at the King's theatre with three of her fellow nursing friends. Casualty was quieter this week as it was the second week off the fair holiday with poor weather so fewer people were about.

Joan would not go down to Arran for a few weeks. Her parents stayed down to the end of August.

During the week, Joan got a letter from Ruth to say that Mr and Mrs Peabody had gone home. A gorgeous looking son had come up in a big posh car and they were able to place Mrs Peabody safely in the back of the car. Also, Ruth's husband was due home at the beginning of August.

Joan still thought about Michael. She had taken a real shine to him. However, she did not want to be a nuisance to ITU. Joan hoped he would soon recover and that he and his mother would move house soon.

In the meantime, Michael had developed a chest infection and requiring antibiotics, was kept in ITU for a few more days. Then he was to be transferred to the orthopaedic ward. His mother visited again in ITU where she found him lying quietly with open eyes. He had a slight smile, when she arrived, on his face. Some of his workmates had visited her when they had heard of his accident, and she related this to him and he nodded his head. Mrs Jones also waived a letter in his face. They had their moving date end of September. So, she told him he had to better, get well, soon. He smiled at her. Michael's general condition was starting to improve and by the end of the week he was ready to go to orthopaedics. His breathing was back to normal and his tracheostomy could be removed. His chest infection was better, so off he went to orthopaedics. ITU would be busy again at the weekend as the holidays were over so the children would be back at school.

Joan met Susan as they were both going to the nurses' home for a few days off. Susan told Joan; Michael had gone to orthopaedics. Susan smiled at Joan's interest but said nothing

Chapter 5

Michael was now in Ward 42, a male orthopaedic ward. His leg was elevated, and he would get daily physiotherapy. When his mother came to visit him, she had another of his workmates with her. Jamie had brought her in his car. Mrs Jones could now explain to Michael that he had to hurry up and get home as they are to move by September weekend, and she did not want to move his things. Jamie asked Michael, if he had any idea why he was attacked. Michael feared it was the drug gang but did not want to speak in front of his mother. Perhaps the police would come to find him. He was so glad they were moving. He must keep away from gangs in the future.

Joan had a good weekend and popped into the ward as the visitors left. Mrs Jones smiled at her and explained to Jamie that she was Michael's nurse in casualty. Whilst Michael and Joan were talking, sister of the ward came up to Joan saying that the senior doctor in casualty wanted to see her. Joan rushed off, waving at Michael. Now what had she done wrong! However, when she reached Doctor Munro's office, he was smiling at her. So, she felt reassured. He asked her to sit down. Doctor Munro has had a call from a local GP, who he trained with to say that they are having an influx of children with 'Lice infestation'. Dr Munro turned to Joan and asked how she was getting on in casualty. She responded that she was enjoying it. He then asked her if she would be prepared to go out to the community to help with this problem he had. She hesitated, looked down and thought about it.

"Would this be permanent?" she asked.

"Oh, no," said the doctor, "just a one off to help out."

The school nurses would help her and she would join them at the worst schools. So, Joan agreed.

Next morning, Joan was given a large box and sent off on the 31 bus, to take her to the clinic nearest to Castlemilk where she would meet the school nurses (known locally as the nitty-gritty nurses). Julia, the nurse in charge was delighted to meet her. She was shown around the clinic and the nurses explained their daily trips to the schools. Would she mind going with someone the first day and then manage on her own. Joan was willing to help in any way possible. This was a real change for her. Although she had learnt about district nursing in her training, she had never been involved with it. So, Joan was to accompany Julie to one of the biggest new schools in Castlemilk. Joan was intrigued because this was where Michael's mother had said they were moving to.

Joan spent the day with Julie. They gave a short talk to the whole school on hygiene and then inspected each class for hair nits; finding many, handed out combs, liquid cleaner and telling each child to take it home and get the whole family involved. They could come to the clinic for more liquid if needed. They should have been excluded from school but as most of the school was affected it would not be in the best interest to school to exclude so many children.

After a busy morning, Julie and Joan went to the local clinic for lunch. As this was a new estate, there were no café shops. Only a few grocers, no leisure places. It was all new and empty. The authorities were only interested in building the high-rise flats to move people into, from the inner city. Much later, shops and even leisure centres would be needed as people from the inner city expected entertainment on their doorsteps. Buses seemed frequent, and so after lunch and a busy afternoon Joan boarded a bus back to her hospital, promising to return the next day. On the bus, Joan sat down next to an elderly lady who turned to her with surprise. She quietly asked Joan if she was a nurse and worked in casualty. Joan was surprised at the voice as she had been dreaming after her busy day. Joan turned to the voice and realised someone was talking to her. Mrs Jones looked familiar but Joan could (at first) not place her.

"Yes," she answered.

Mrs Jones said, "You cared for my boy."

Suddenly, Joan remembered her. Mrs Jones thanked Joan and said, she had seen Michael in his new ward. Now she was on her way home after viewing their new flat, 10 storeys up. It was nice, but a long way from home. She would tell Michael all about it when she would see him later tonight. Joan sent Michael her regards as Mrs Jones left the bus. Now Joan started to think of Michael. Should she visit him in the ward or what?

Chapter 6

Michael got home on Friday and as Joan was off on Wednesday and Thursday, she did not see him before he left. Casualty was now busy again with quite a few people who needed interpreters so it took longer to deal with them. This waste frustrating for the nursing staff and doctors as they had to wait for the interpreters to come from their offices. This caused delays and frustrations for all. So, the senior doctor was asked to see if they could get a permanent translator in casualty. The next time Joan was off, she decided to go and see her parents; now home in King's Park. Perhaps she would mention Michael to her mother. In the meantime, Michael was home, sorting out his room and preparing to return to work. He was not sure how he was going to manage his job as a liner off but hoped his boss would be kind to him until he would be fit again. Michael had been the best apprentice in his year and was generally well liked so hopefully they would be kind to him.

Life seemed to settle down for Michael and Joan. So, one night, Michael sat down to write to Joan. It was a brief note asking her to go to the cinema with him. He suggested they would meet in town at the cinema in Sauchiehall Street at 7.00 p.m. and perhaps a meal before the film.

Joan was delighted to hear from Michael and wrote quickly back agreeing. It was the Wednesday after she had been home and told her mother about Michael so she was excited. What should she wear? Did she have time to have her hair done? Her friend, Susan, said she would help her get ready as she knew Michael from her nightshift in ITU. So together they found a nice bright summer dress in Joan's wardrobe with matching shoes and jacket. Susan lent her a bag and put her hair up for her. Michael only told his mother, not to make dinner for him as after a good wash he was going out. His mother said do not be too late you have work in the morning. So, the two met up and had a lovely time together eating, talking and seeing a film. Michael even saw Joan back to the nurses' home and jumped into a taxi back to Govan. Not too expensive but would not be possible if and when he and his mother moved.

Joan had just reached her room, when she heard the home's phone and as she did not know who would ring the home at this time of night, she ran to answer it. Just as well as it was her mother to say her father had been rushed to the Victoria infirmary with intense pain, possibly a kidney stone (the ambulance driver had said). Joan told her mother she would meet her there. A taxi took Joan quickly to the Southside, and she had money in her purse as Michael had paid for everything. When she got to casualty, she found her mother in the waiting room. Michael came and got her as they knew what had happened to her husband. Just as Joan sat down, a nurse came and said she and her mother could come through to see her father and husband. Joan's father was lying on a bed with the curtains drawn. He looked pale but not in pain. He had been given an injection of painkillers and was waiting to find out what was to happen next. He told Joan he had been feeling squeamish for a few days, but this evening he suddenly got this awful pain and asked her mother to call 999.

Soon an older man, a doctor came around the curtains and told them that Mr Hughes would be going to the surgical ward for possible surgery. They could wait and go up to the ward with him – this they did. Mrs Hughes and Joan were left waiting outside the ward while the staff admitted Mr Hughes. Mrs Hughes held Joan's hand and thanked her for coming so quickly. Joan wondered if she should call in sick for her shift next morning but decided to see what would happen now. Soon the nurse called Angela, came out and said they could see Mr Hughes for a few minutes. He was going to theatre shortly, as luckily he had not eaten since early evening. Joan and her mother spent a few minutes with him and left the staff to prepare Mr Hughes for his operation. Angela gave them the phone Number and told them they could phone in the morning. Joan asked her mother whether she should go home with her or not. Mrs Hughes told Joan to go back to her nurses' home and go on duty next morning. Joan gave her mother the casualty number, where she could phone Joan in the morning. They kissed goodbye and went their own way.

Joan was not only overtired with all the events of the night but concerned about her dad.

Joan could not remember either of her parents being ill. However, she made herself a cup of Cocoa and settled down to get some sleep. Next day after her shift, Joan made her way; by bus to Victoria to see her father. He was perky, sitting up in bed entertaining the surrounding patients. Shortly, Joan's mother appeared. They sat comfortably around the bed. Joan said she was getting bored in casualty and would like to get into a ward. However, there were no vacancies in the Royal Infirmary. Joan's mother carefully suggested the Victoria, and to come and live at home. Joan said she would think about it. She had not yet told her parents about Michael and his move to Castlemilk. After a while, Joan got up saying good-bye to her parents and wandered over to the nurses' desk. She asked one of the nurses about staff vacancies in the hospital. One nurse said she had heard that they were planning to open a coronary care ward to split from ITU. Perhaps, Joan would fancy that. She left the ward and got a bus back to the Royal where there had been a call for her. It was Michael to say they were moving and hoped to get a telephone. He would ring as soon as he could. Joan had a lot to think about now. Joan was meeting Susan after her night shift as Joan was not on duty until 1.00 p.m. Susan breezed in, laughing to herself. She had a great story for Joan. They sat in Joan's room with the summer-late sun streaming in. Susan began. Last Night, she was delegated to the surgical block so went via the tunnels as it was pouring with rain. As she approached the corridor to the mortuary, she saw what looked like a pair eyes watching her. She dashed back to the office and got the night superintendent to come with her. Susan was quite scared now. When they got to the mortuary corridor, they called out and something moved and got up. Susan nearly ran away. It was a man. He explained he was a junior doctor who had no accommodation until he was due at the end of the month. It was the 30th today. The superintendent told him off for frightening her nurse and for using the hospital property for his convenience. Why did he sleep with his eyes open? He had not been asleep and tried to talk to Susan but she was so frightened she had run away. The superintendent sent the young doctor up to the doctors' sleepover room and told him to report to the medical superintendent next morning. Susan was sent on her Rounds but said she would brave the rain on her return to the night office. Joan and Susan had a good laugh then.

Joan now explained to Susan her latest problem. Should she go to the Victoria infirmary and live at home. Also, it was nearer her new friend Michael. What should she do? They discussed it and Susan said, "Why not take the chance of a new project and save some money by staying at home?"

Joan agreed and made an appointment to see Matron. So, Susan went off to bed and Joan went to get an appointment with Matron and then went on duty. Later that week Michael phoned her to say they were moving and he would phone with his new number. Joan did not mention her plans on the phone. Michael had a friend whose uncle worked at house removals company so he would move them. Michael's mother was all excited.

Chapter 7

Joan went to see Matron who was most encouraging. Joan needed to contact the Matron of the Victoria before she gave in her notice to the Royal. This she did and got an interview shortly. In the meantime, she said nothing at work but went to see her parents. Her father was home and doing well. Her mother was delighted with her news and was planning to freshen up her room. Now she waited for Michael to call with his new phone number to tell her all. Next day, Michael phoned and firstly gave her his new number and then asked her out. Joan was delighted as she had lots to tell him. At work the talk was all about a Christmas dance at the Grosvenor hotel at central station. Joan was going to ask Michael to go with her. In the meantime, Michael was busy moving from the Gorbals to Castlemilk. He had to leave earlier in the morning to get to work on time. One Monday morning, he was called to his boss's office. He was not pleased as he knew his boss would be in a bad mood. The boss was an Ardent Celtic supporter as ardent as Michael was a Rangers man. The two teams had played at the weekend and Rangers had won away from home. However, Michael braced himself for the meeting. Knocking on the office door a voice called out sharply, "Come." Into the fiery den he went. The boss indicated a chair. Michael sat down cautiously and waited. The boss did not waste time with pleasantries. He said, "Michael we have a new job for you." Michael looked up.

"Yes," he said.

"There is to be a new planning department to be set up," said the boss. "We would like you to join it."

A step up for Michael with more money, not to be refused. So, Michael nodded his head and said, "When?"

The boss said, "At the end of this month." He then got up and went out pleased with the meeting.

Now he must ring Joan tonight and arrange to see her. Perhaps they can get closer now his worries were ebbing away. He still had some stiffness in his leg but now that he would not be going up and down to the ship hopefully it would improve. In the yard the mood was grim.

There was talk of a strike over the boilermakers' demarcation and there was a ship soon for launching. Michael did not want a strike as no money came in, and he had a new rent to pay in the new flat. Michael often felt that he went one step forward and two back. A new job but a threatened strike. However, he decided to phone Joan and arranged to see her. Perhaps a nice meal somewhere in the Southside. Joan was in her room when a friend came to say there was a call for her. She ran down the stairs. It was Michael in great form.

"Yes, I will meet you at the Old Mill in Cathcart," she said, "at 7 p.m."

Joan ran upstairs to get dressed and met Susan on her way for a bath, before going on night duty. Joan quickly told Susan she was off out with Michael again. Susan was pleased for her.

Susan and Michael met in the Indian restaurant down from the Victoria hospital. They both had a lot to tell each other but first they ordered their meal. The owners knew Joan from her visits with her parents and knew what she liked to eat. Michael had never eaten Indian food so he took advice from Joan as he gazed into her eyes. He was fascinated by her.

Once their food was on the table, they were ready to talk. "You first," said Michael to Joan. Firstly, she asked Michael to come to the nurses' ball at the big Grosvenor Hotel at the central station. Michael was a little surprised, and in awe. He had never been to a ball.

Of course, he agreed and asked when it was so that he could prepare for it. It was to be in late December before Christmas. Then Joan broke the next news. She was hoping to move hospitals to a new unit being set up in the Victoria Hospital. It would mean moving back home to her parents' house, but she was sick of the nurses' home and fed up with casualty. Michael took all this in and wondered if their relationship was moving on.

"Your turn now," said Joan to Michael. They had finished most of their meal and were drinking coffee. Michael told her about the immediate strike by the boilermakers which he hoped would not affect the whole work as he would not get paid if he was on strike, and he had just got a new rent. He also told about his promotion, which pleased her a lot as she knew he was struggling with the climbing after his leg injury.

After a good meal and chat, they both felt happier and left the restaurant smiling.

Michael reached out to Joan and pecked her on the cheek saying, "Let's look forward with hope." Joan was happy and on returning to the hospital she phoned her parents with the news. Her mother was delighted that she was coming home

Chapter 8

Michael was back at work when a scaffolder fell and died. All the workers walked out but Michael suggested that instead of walking out, the men should give a day's wages to the widow. So, he lost a day's wages and the boilermakers were disputing with the carpenters and threatening strike action. This was all Michael needed in his new job in the planning department. One morning on his way to college, he met Jamie. He thanked him for his help with his mother when Michael was in hospital. Jamie was also unhappy about the possible strike as he wanted to get engaged to his girlfriend and was saving for the ring. They were both trying so hard to improve their lot. One step forward and two back, Michael kept on thinking.

However, to lighten their mood. They had a good laugh when a frigate for India was launched by the Indian high commissioner with a coconut.

At college, Michael was studying for his HND—Higher National Diploma in Marine Sanitary Engineering—which might help him in the future. He dearly liked to become a draftsman and get into the drawing office. In the meantime, the boilermakers had meetings after meetings and eventually an all-out strike.

Michael tried to phone Joan to see if they could meet during the day whilst he was off work. However, when Joan went back to work the consultant in charge of casualty knew about her resignation and was not pleased so he put her on night duty. This is often done when one angers the boss! Joan was really upset but knew it was only for a few weeks until she left the Royal infirmary. She eventually heard from Michael that she could not see him during the day. They were both sad but looked forward to the ball. It was going to be a great night. Joan's mother had promised to go with her to get an evening dress in Glasgow. So, on one of her night off they went into town and looked for dress. They found a lovely dress, and it fitted Joan perfectly. Then her mother took her for lunch. So, they had a good day together. Winter was in full fling, and it was cold and wet but luckily no snow yet. Joan did not want snow before the ball. In the meantime, Michael was using saved money to buy a suit for the ball. Luckily, he had only lost four days with the strike because work needed to be on going for the forthcoming launch in the spring.

Joan was having a hard time on night duty as she was not a good sleeper at the best of times, and she was sad at saying good-bye to her many friends at the Royal. But she knew it was for the best. Also, she would be saving money, staying at home. Life went on, and Joan was getting excited about the ball and her parents had asked her to invite Michael and his mother for Christmas day. Joan had picked to be off on Christmas and work New Year. All staff did one or the other.

Next time Michael phoned Joan and asked her for Christmas and they arranged to go for a drink before the dance. He said he would speak to his mother. He expected she would agree as she was missing her old friends in the Gorbals. So, Mrs Stone was delighted with the invite.

What should she take to the Hughes house? She would bake some shortbread and a bun. Michael could get the drink so all was arranged.

The ball was magnificent all decorated in Christmas twinkles with lavish food and drink. Joan introduced Michael to her friends. He recognised Susan from his hospital stay.

Michael was a good dancer, and Joan had had lessons as a teenager so they made a great pair. Admiration was on Michael's face and Joan was very happy smiling away. Michael did not want to burst Joan's bubble but he was worried about the future as the upcoming launch was the last ship on order for the yard. There was talk of people leaving and going abroad but this was not an option Michael would consider with his mother aging and his involvement with Joan. Perhaps he could move to another shipyard for getting his HND, or he could go up to the drawing office somewhere else?

In the meantime, he kept these thoughts to himself. Michael and Joan arranged to meet at his parents' house on Christmas day. Joan had brought Michael a shirt from strumps in town.

Michael had found a nice necklace with a small ship on it in a jeweller's shop in Shawlands and was pleased with himself. Lucky by now, the shipyards no longer worked Christmas day so Michael was off for a week until after Hogmanay. So now, Joan was off Christmas but would work on nights over New Year. Joan's father collected her on Christmas morning, and Michael with his mother came by taxi. They had a lovely day. Mrs Stone and Mrs Hughes got on well, and Mr Hughes and Michael had lots to talk about as Joan's dad had been a plumber trained in the yard where Michael worked. The day passed quickly with a lovely meal of turkey with all the trimmings and plum pudding. Michael had brought some wine too.

So, Mr Hughes decided to take everyone home. Joan thanked her parents for a lovely day and so did Michael and his mother. Michael and Joan arranged to meet before Hogmanay as Joan was on nights on the 30th, 31st 1st and 2nd. Michael was off until the 6th of January. Then he would be busy with the forthcoming launch. Joan would leave the Royal infirmary at the end of January with two weeks' holiday before she would start in the Victoria. Both Michael and Joan were uptight when they met before the New Year. The next year would be changing things, and Michael was anxious about committing himself with Joan as he feared he would lose his job when the last ship on the order books would be launched and he did not know what the future held.

Joan was thinking of the new challenge in the new unit in the Victoria and moving away from her friends. So, they had a quiet lunch and went off their own ways.

Chapter 9

Joan went on duty on Hogmanay, feeling on edge as this was a difficult time in casualty and it seemed very windy outside. Joan dealt with a few drunks and talked to her friends. Michael tried to phone her before she went on duty but the nurses' home's phone was very busy. Suddenly in the middle of the night the staff in casualty heard roaring outside. They opened the outside door and nearly got pulled out. There was a gale blowing. A call came in from the police to warn off strong, gale force winds knocking things down and blowing things all over the place. Up in the surgical and medical blocks the buildings were swaying and the Staff moved all the patients into the centre of the wards. Outside it was getting worse people staying in the tenements opposite the hospital were so frightened that they came to casualty out of fear. Tiles were flying everywhere and people had already been hit. The ambulances were roaring in with casualties, and Joan was kept busy. Suddenly, all the lights went out. The emergency generators kicked in but did not last. All surgery had been stopped and casualties were redirected to Stobhill outside Glasgow. Now Joan and her team opened the doors to see devastation all over the courtyard outside the casualty department. In the wards, some patients had even been sick with the sawing of the buildings. When the electricity came back on, the ambulances starting rushing in people with cuts and bruising from flying glass, and tiles.

It became a hectic night. By the time morning came, Joan and her staff were exhausted. They were told they would be taken home, if necessary, by taxi as there did not seem to be any buses. Joan was glad she was still in the nurses' home and hurried to her room and bed.

Sleeping like a log, she was woken by a banging on her door. It was one of the day nurses to tell her there was a phone call for her. She quickly pulled on her dressing gown and went to the phone. It was Michael to see if she was okay. He said, "Their block swayed but no damage was done, but Glasgow looked as if it had been in a war." She had not phoned her parents so she quickly rang off from Michael and phoned her parents. Mr Hughes answered the phone and was delighted to hear from his daughter. They had slept through the storm but round about them, there was a lot of damage with fallen trees. Even the lone piper who serenaded their street could not come out this Hogmanay What a start to the New Year. Now, Joan was preparing to leave the nurses' home and move home. Her dad was helping her as she had been in the nurses' home for years now. Mum had her room redecorated and was eagerly awaiting her daughter's return home.

Michael was busy at work wondering what would happen when the ship would launch. Where would he go? Some men were already looking at going abroad or to the naval yard. Michael's new boss was nice and told him to hold on and that he would try to get him into Fairfield's drawing office. His boss was ready to retire so he was quite happy at the closing of the yard. There was a feeling of anticipation in the whole place. The weather after the storm was now cold and wet; really dry winter weather. However, spring was coming. Michael had asked Joan to the launch and hopefully if he knew where, he was going he would see about an engagement ring. One day, he phoned Joan's dad and asked him to meet him for a drink. Mr Hughes thought he knew what was coming and was pleased to meet Michael. They met up one evening and Michael told Mr Hughes of his plans. At last things were going well. However, Michael's mother had a terrible cough and Michael tried to persuade her to see a doctor. She had not yet registered with a new practice since their move so Michael took a half day off, and they went to register with the local practice. It was in a nice new building and very pleasant. Also, the doctors; all seemed young and helpful. Mrs Stone was quite happy. The doctor ordered an X-ray and took blood, giving her a cough bottle. She was to return in 10 days' time for the results.

At the beginning of the new month, February, Michael was told he would be able to go to Fairfield after the launch. He was delighted and phoned Joan who was just about to leave the Royal. The staff in casualty had a farewell tea for her and were all sorry to see her go. She had a week off before starting at the Victoria, so intended to rest after the tiring night duty, and to see Michael.

Chapter 10

Joan was settled at home with her parents. Michael had asked her to go with him to the launch so she was ready to start anew in the Victoria. Matron had welcomed her and shown her around the new unit, meeting the staff. One of the senior staff nurses remembered Joan from the Royal when Joan was a student nurse. She was especially nice to Joan. Her name was Sandra. So, a new life was beginning. To start with, Joan had to undergo an induction course of one week. So, she worked 9-5 each day. Oh, it was a relief to be off nights. Michael and Joan met during this week and Michael explained about the forthcoming launch. At present, the ship would have a number but would be named by someone special. They did not know who yet. Michael told Joan to arrive early as there would be a big queue, as this was the last ship of the shipyard. People would be happy and sad. Some of them knew where they were going, but a few had no future. Some of Michael's Friends were going to Canada or Australia but Michael was happy to go to Fairfield and stay in Glasgow.

Now the day of the launch approached. Joan arrived early as Michael told her to. There was already a small queue but it was a sunny dry day. As the time of the launch, Michael appeared at Joan's side and the doors opened. Michael told Joan where to stand, so he would meet her later at that point. Off he went with a skip in his step as this would be a special day for him if she agreed. He had her father's permission and the ring in his pocket. The band played and up on the stand stood all the dignitaries ready for the launch. It was as if Princess Alexandre who was launching the ship. A service was held prior to the launch. The band had stopped playing and her voice rang out, "I launch this ship, Port Caroline, may

God bless her and all who sail in her." A big roar went out. The chains pulled the ship into the water. All went well. Then suddenly Michael was by Joan's side. He showed her around the yard which had been tidied up for the launch. He took her to the planning office and explained how he was moving to Fairfield as the work was finished here, and everyone was going places. Michael said he could have gone abroad but only said he could not leave his mother, especially as she had not been well lately. They went for a cup of tea in the canteen and then Michael took her out for dinner. They went to 'Singers', a restaurant that Michael knew as some of his schoolmates who had worked at the Singer's factory often went there. They were seated in a corner booth and looked at the menu. Michael dug in his pocket and found the box. He slowly brought it out and facing Joan said, "Please, will you marry me?" dipping down on one knee, he looked up at her.

She smiled at him and said with a twinkle in her eyes, "Yes." They shook hands, and Michael gave her a peck on the check. Other diners saw what was going on and clapped their hands and shouted "Good Luck" to them. Now it was time for a celebratory meal. A couple in the next booth sent over a bottle of wine, and Michael and Joan toasted each other with it. This was quite a day for them. After a good meal of starters of prawn cocktail, they had a dish of real ale pie with roast potatoes and mixed vegetables. Finishing up with ice-cream For Michael, and cheese and biscuits for Joan. Followed by tea and coffee. A lovely end to a great day. Smiling at everybody, they left holding hands and went on their way home. They were able to get the same bus most of the way.

Joan ran into her parents' house smiling and calling, "Mum, Dad, guess what." Dad was already prepared as Michael had already spoken to him. They both kissed Joan and were pleased for her. Michael got home to find his mother lying on the couch looking pale and worn.

He gently touched her and she sprung up.

"Oh sorry," she said. Michael was only concerned for her. They sat down and Michael made a cup of tea before telling her his news. She was delighted as she had grown to like Joan and her family. She knew that Michael would now be taken care of when she was no longer there. So, life could go on and Michael would be okay. Mrs Stone had been worrying about the future as she knew she was not well. She asked when the wedding would be but Michael and Joan had not yet discussed it but he said they are not teenagers and did not intend waiting too long. They would have to look for accommodation convenient to both their works, on a good bus route. So, it would have to be in the south side of Glasgow. Buying a flat would not be possible as the bank would only take Michael's wage in consideration and it was much less than Joan's.

So, they would need to rent in the meantime. They looked around but most places were either too expensive or not nice. It depressed them. However, Joan's parents said they would try and help.

Chapter 11

Michael's mother was not well at all. He took her to the doctor again who looked serious and asked all sorts of questions including was she eating. Mrs Stone had lost a lot of weight and was very pale. The doctor took blood samples and listened to her chest, recommending a chest X-ray. As the doctor put his stethoscope away, he looked up at Michael and shook his head. Then Michael and his mother left the surgery and went home.

Michael told Joan that night what the doctor had implied. Joan had already feared the worst when she last saw Mrs Stone looking so pale and thin. However, she did not want to frighten Michael.

Joan was reasonably happy living at home but missed her nursing friends. The job is going well and she saw more of Michael now as she was not on night duty. Now Michael was getting more and more worried about his mother and persuaded her to go back to the doctor. However, all the doctor did was offer a cough bottle and suggest help from the social services. Mrs Stone was outraged and left the surgery in high dudgeon. So, there was nothing Michael could do. Michael told Joan all this on their next night out. Joan gently suggested that perhaps they should think of bringing the wedding forward. Michael smiled at Joan and relaxed for a bit.

"Oh, what a good idea," he said, smiling at his fiancée. Michael's mother knew the end was coming and was relieved when Michael told her that they were going to try and bring the wedding forward. Michael's mother also told Michael to look after himself for his new life. Michael thanked his mother for her concern and asked Joan to speak to her parents about rearranging the wedding.

Joan's parents were happy to rearrange things and quickly got in touch with the minister, the 'Beechwood' and sent out new invitations. Joan was busy at work learning new procedures for cardiac patients and looking forward to her wedding. Hoping Mrs Stone would make it. Michael was settling down in the drawing office. So perhaps things were looking up in Glasgow and after the wedding they would be able to find a house of their own. Michael spent as much time as he could with his mother. Joan asked Michael to come to her parents' house next Sunday to discuss new wedding plans. So, Michael went for lunch the next Sunday, and they sorted out the plans for the wedding to take place at the beginning of July not at the fair holiday. Michael would need to see his boss to get time off and to rearrange his honeymoon plans.

So, on Monday morning, Michael approached his new boss in the drawing office. He appeared a reasonable man and was delighted for Michael, giving a pat on the back and said, "Go ahead, young man, arrange with personal for your time off." Michael was happy to tell Joan all was set. Michael went next Saturday to the travel agent to book the honeymoon which was to be in Madeira. His friends had recommended it as a great place for a honeymoon as the 'lager louts' did not go there. Also, many of the hotels were 'Adult only'.

Michael decided to tell his mother his plans. She was delighted to hear all was going well. She decided to get her friend Daisy and go into town for a new outfit. So, one day when she felt quite good they went into town by bus, and got a nice pale blue outfit in one of the Stores and then treated themselves to lunch. Michael was pleased to see his mother brighter and happy with herself about the forthcoming wedding. Now everything was coming together.

Chapter 12

Joan and her mother started to make plans for a wedding.
Michael had confided in Joan that his mother was not well and
would like the wedding sooner than later. They would need to
find a church and make arrangements. So, one day Michael
came over, after work, to Joan's parents' house to discuss
wedding plans. Joan's mother suggested their local church
and as Michael was not a churchgoer so he was in agreement.
He did say that they did not want as he had no relatives
besides his mother. He was an only child and so were his
parents. A few distant cousins lived abroad in America and
Canada. Joan's dad was one of four brothers, all in Glasgow
and Joan's mother had one sister in Glasgow. So, Joan and
Michael had an appointment with the minister of Joan's
parents' church in King's Park. Now Joan and her mother
could think of clothes and her father would find a venue which
was easy for him. His local 'The Beechwood' would be ideal.
So, once the couple would have a venue, a date could be set
up. Michael told his mother of their plans when he brought
Joan up the next Saturday. The date-set for their wedding was
to be July 15th Fair Friday as Michael would be able to take
the day off and have the honeymoon over the fair holidays.
Joan had a friend whose mother, Lindsey in Ayrshire would
do the wedding invitations, order of service and favours etc.
Now it was time for Joan and her mother to get started on the
dresses. Joan had asked Michael to wear a kilt and her uncles
would do the same.

The Banns were raised and Joan and Michael met the
minister. They chose hymns, number 23 and 121. The
organist met them too. The church would be decorated by the

guild as Joan's mother was a member. Joan wanted a pale pink everywhere and in her bouquet.

Now Joan and her mother could go into town on Joan's day off to look for a dress. Joan had asked Ruth in Arran to be her best maid. Michael would ask Jamie to be his best man. So, things were progressing well. Joan was enjoying her work in the Victoria hospital. All was settling down in Michael's work. The only fly on the wall was Michael's mother who still had this awful cough which made her very breathless. However, she was very happy that Michael had found a lovely girl. Perhaps his life would now be better. No more gangs, she hoped. Joan and her mother went into town to look for a dress. They went to the big stores first and then went to wedding dress shops. Joan had seen a dress she liked in a magazine. It was plain at the top with a full skirt, long sleeves finishing in a V at the cuffs. The skirt also finished in a V and was mid length. All in a brocade white. Eventually they found a dress they liked in Frasers. The sales girl was so helpful and the dress fitted without any alteration needed. It was also not too pricey as Joan was determined to pay for it but her mother insisted she was buying it. So, after a debate, Joan agreed. Now they went off for lunch and a nice quiet sit down. Although there were still lots to do things were falling into place.

The summer was coming. A wedding was set. So, all was well for the two families. As it was a lunchtime wedding, they did not need a band. All they had to do now was decide on the numbers for the 'Beechwood' restaurant. Joan and her mother discussed this over lunch. Joan did not want a big affair but family and friends needed to be invited. Joan wanted friends from the 'Royal' as well as one or two from her present work. Her mother naturally wanted her relatives as Joan was an only child.

Now they would have to ask Michael, whom he wanted. So, on the next night Joan and Michael met, they discussed numbers. Michael had a few friends from work and college but no relations in Scotland, and he did not expect those abroad to come but would send out invitations. Now Joan got in touch with Lindsey in Ayrshire with her numbers and went with her parents down one day to order the invitations and see the other things for the big day. It was all ready, and Joan was delighted with everything.

Chapter 13

The wedding was drawing near and everything was set. Michael was trying to keep his mother going, and Joan was all set with a lovely white long dress and veil with roses and other flowers through the silk material. Her mother had a pale blue dress and Michael's mother had a pale grey suit. The men were all in Stewart Tartan kilts. Lindsey had all the Accessories, favours etc. ready at the 'Beechwood'. When Joan's mother went to check everything, she was delighted with it all. The cars had been ordered. The 'Banns' had gone out. So, the big day arrived. Joan had her make-up Done by one of the girls from the 'Royal' and the hairdresser came to the house.

So, Joan and Michael tied the knot in the church and went for the luncheon in the 'Beechwood'. Michael had not told Joan that the honeymoon was in Madeira. So, when the taxi arrived to take them to the airport Joan had on a lovely yellow suit and was pleased to hear they were flying off to a warm place. Everyone wished them well. The luncheon had been good and everything flowed smoothly. Everyone gathered outside as the 'Old Car' drew up with all the trimmings rattling at the back. Michael had change in his pocket to throw out the window whilst Joan threw her bouquet to be caught by a friend of hers, Susan from the 'Royal'. On the way to the airport, Michael told Joan they were going to Madeira. Joan was delighted as she had heard good reports of that island. Michael had booked them into the 'Adults only' hotel with a sea view and balcony. The flight was four hours.

Time for the young marrieds to settle down after their hectic day. Life was looking up, and Michael was now more cheerful but still worried about his mother. However, he should put thoughts of her out of his mind and look after his new wife

Chapter 14

Now, Michael was involved with the disputes at work and very worried about the future. Joan was reasonably happy at work but also worried about Michael. He still had to settle his late mother's flat and needed a day off to empty the flat; returning the keys to the housing people as well as dealing with other things regarding his late mother's affairs. What should he do?

Winter was coming and they still did not have a real home of their own. Although there was no problem of them staying in the flat but they had to pay the rent. It made it hard for them to save for their own place. Life was not easy. Who said it was?

Joan was busy at work one day, when she experienced a sharp pain in her side and collapsed on the floor. Immediately the other nurses were at her side. They lifted her onto a spare bed as she came around. One of the junior doctors was in the ward and quickly came over to her.

Joan was pale, sweating and in obvious pain. Her pulse was racing and her blood pressure was through the roof. The doctor, Jack, examined Joan finding her stomach hard and sore to touch. Jack turned to sister with the words, "I believe we have an appendix here, sister." David, a senior registered, entered the ward and was shown Joan who was awake but very pale in a lot of pain. David examined her and suggested they move her to the surgical ward for theatre as soon as possible. Joan tried to apologise for all the fuss but sister waved her way to the surgical ward. Everyone told her not to worry they would contact her husband and parents. Luckily, they found a slot and Joan had her operation at 3 p.m. Michael got leave to come to the hospital where he met Joan's parents.

They were shown into a side room where Joan lay out for a count and did not realise she had visitors. Sister told them all had gone well and they should return for evening visit. The staff nurse in this ward remembered Joan from her time at the 'Royal'.

When Joan woke up, she smiled at the nurse. Then Joan remembered Mary and asked her to help her to ready for visiting time. Joan was given some pain relief before her husband and parents came in. They were all pleased to see Joan lying quietly and stayed a short while only as Joan was falling off to sleep again, the best cure. Joan slept well and felt much stronger next morning, managing her breakfast. Joan was able to get up and was hoping to be discharged. She recommended that perhaps it would be a good idea if Joan went to her parents for a few days as Michael was out all day. Joan thought this over and asked Michael how he reacts about it. He agreed and Joan's parents told him to come over each evening for his meal and see Joan. So, they all agreed with sister and in a few days Joan went to her parents' home. Joan was soon on her feet again and ready to go back to their flat with Michael. Michael had sorted out all his late mother's business and was pleased to tell Joan his mother had left them some money. However, he did not say much to Joan about things at work.

Chapter 15

Michael came home in a down mood to find Joan busy in the kitchen. He bent to give her a kiss and she told him to wash his hands and sit down, dinner would be ready soon. Joan had made Michael's favourite meal. Mince and tatties (Potatoes) followed by ice-cream and jelly. Soon the dinner appeared on the small table with a jug of water. They ate their meal quietly. Michael trying to work out how to tell Joan about the problems at work. Eventually Joan cleared the table and they sat down with their tea before the TV, but it was not on. Michael asked Joan how she felt, and she said she was fine and going back to work next week. Then Michael started to tell her about work. The draughtsmen in Swan and Hunter's in Newcastle were in dispute with the management and the problems were escalating to Glasgow. Joan asked what it meant to them. Michael said there was talk of a 'Lock out' which he explained meant no wages, only union money. Joan looked up at his worried face and told him not to worry; she had been paid full wages whilst off sick and would be back at work next week. Michael was still not sure how long this dispute would last as the ship they were building (Port Caroline) was in early stages and the draughtsmen were heavily involved. Joan and Michael went early to bed and Joan again told Michael to stop worrying; they would manage and could always call on her parents. It took Michael a while to fall asleep as he thought about some of his mates who had gone abroad but how he could with Joan, Still close to her parents?

Next day at work Michael found himself and the rest of the drawing office 'Locked Out'. So, home he went. Now he really was down. If he had no wages coming in how could they pay the rent and even think about a house for themselves. Life was really getting tough. Also, the winter was coming; it was dark in the morning and early dark at night. Michael tried to have a meal ready for Joan when she came home quite tired after her time off work. Michael had to report for picket duty every few days but nothing was happening and Michael was really down. He tried to put a smile on his face when Joan came in tired from work. Joan had news for him. She was to do a stint on nights. Not her chose but extra money for them. So, they would plod on with Michael looking forward to the football and Joan bracing herself for night duty; not her favourite job. Perhaps she will need to find something else soon.

The weekend came, Michael went off to the match as Joan got up readying herself for nights. A Saturday night it would be busy. Joan sat down with the television on, drinking a cup of tea. On the TV, there was a picture of a grass field. Joan did not take much notice until the phone rang. She turned the TV down and answered the phone to her father. All he said, very agitated, was, "Michael at the match."

"Of course," said Joan. Then her dad told her there had been a terrible accident at Ibrox. As people were exiting the stands, there was a sudden about turn as a final goal was called and the stairs collapsed, crushing many people. Joan did not know what to do. Dad said he would come over to her and they would wait for Michael, hopefully, to come home. Michael was often known to walk to and from Ibrox so they would just have to wait and see. On the 6.00 p.m. news, it was announced that there had been a severe accident at a football match in Glasgow but details were still coming in. At about 6.30 p.m., Michael rang the doorbell and Joan and her dad jumped to it. Michael was astounded at the not know of the tragedy as he had left before the last whistle and by a rear door. He wandered about some of his mates but all he could do was reassure his father-in-law and his wife. Joan's dad went off home then, and Joan made Michael's tea before getting ready to go to work. She left Michael on the phone to his mates and reported for night duty.

The word at work was that there were so many injuries that the Victoria would get some patients. So, Joan and Ailsa prepared the unit for them. Soon they came; three very poorly young men. One in particular, was given to Joan. He was wrapped in a Celtic scarf and could hardly breathe. He needed to be ventilated and was very frightened. Joan found out his name was Billy, and she did her best to reassure him and tell him he was safe.

He mumbled, "Did we win?"

Joan felt she had to lie (the score had been nil each). So, she nodded her head to Billy. Within minutes, he struggled to breathe and the ventilator's alarm went off. He had gone. Joan struggled on for the rest of the night. The other two patients survived the night and were there. Joan eventually went off duty. She was shattered and when she got home she collapsed on the setting Michael that she felt she had failed Billy and told a lie. Michael tried to reassure her and sent her to bed with a stiff drink. However, she could not settle thinking of poor Billy. Michael had found all his mates safe. Eventually, Joan fell into a deep sleep and would face the unit again the coming night. One more night and then two weeks holiday.

So next morning, Joan went home singing to herself. Michael was also back at work and she was off for two whole weeks. Suddenly the phone rang. It was an old friend from her training days, Kate. They talked a bit about what they were doing and eventually Kate came to the point of her call. Was Joan free for four nights? Joan sighed but listened to Kate. Kate worked as an industrial nurse at Chryslers in Linwood and needed a night nurse for this week. Joan thought about it quickly and decided it would do her no harm, and she had nothing planned for her holidays, so she agreed. Kate asked her to meet her at the gate at 7.30 p.m. Joan quickly got herself off the bed and was up to tell Michael her news when he came in from work. He was pleased as it would not only give Joan something new but would be extra money for their savings. Joan wondered if this could be a new venture for her. As the Victoria was beginning to get her down. Also, industry paid much better than the NHS. So off Joan went to meet Kate. She was anxious but excited too. Kate was at the gate to meet her. They walked together to the medical cabin talking all the way. At the door to the medical cabin Kate brought out a bunch of keys. Opened the door to reveal a fully equipped medical room. Joan was surprised at all the equipment and looked around in amazement.

Kate explained why she had needed someone immediately. The night nurse had to be dismissed on Friday and the company insisted a nurse was present at all night and day shifts. Luckily there had been no work on Sunday night. Kate just said the night nurse had been dismissed for 'Misbehaviour'. Now Kate went on to explain the workings of a night shift nurse. Security and first-aids were always around. There was a buzzer under the desk, and they would be there at once. Then Kate showed Joan how to record all visits to the medical room, i.e. name, place of work, injury and outcome in a large book kept on the desk. Kate told Joan about the procedure for serious injuries and how the union had to be told if someone needed further medical care or needed to leave the premises. Now Kate asked Joan if she had any questions before she left and would be in at 7.00 a.m.

Joan settled herself down checking the resus equipment and wandering around the room. The phone rang, it was the security officer to say he would be in to see her later but if she had any problems call him on his mobile. All the numbers were up on the board. Suddenly, there was a loud banging on the door Joan went cautiously to open the door. There stood two heavy looking men.

"Where is Alice," one said.

Joan replied, "Not on, tonight." They smirked and walked away. Joan wondered to herself what had been going on. Soon a few more men came mostly with lame excuses to see who she was. She dealt with them putting each one into the book. Eventually, a first aider popped in, and she offered him a cup of tea and he told her what had been going on. The nurse had been fraternising with the men! So, she might get more visitors! Joan laughed; she was a married woman and did not mix work with free time. The first aider got a call and went off. Joan started to read a nursing magazine lying on the desk before the next visit of the security man. He was a nice chap who was an ex-policeman. He told her that there was usually little trouble at night but she would need to be aware of the union guys who would push to keep men working at all costs. However, once the security man left it became a quiet night and Joan had filed in a few minor injuries in the book by 7.00 a.m. when Kate reappeared. Joan told her all that had happened and agreed to do the next three nights.

Chapter 16

On the final morning of her four nights, Joan was really quite used to the job and wondered if there was a future in it for her. Whilst she was tidying up after her shift, Kate came in.

"Good morning, Joan," she said. "Could I persuade you to come her on a more permanent basis?" she asked.

Joan's face lit up. "Oh yes," she immediately replied but then realised that she had a job already. However, she told Kate she would need a month to sort her present job out. Kate said she would get an agency nurse if she could rely on Joan. Joan said, of course and would be in touch as soon as she had sorted things out. Off Joan went with a happy heart. Although it would mean staying on nights but with the extra money, she and Michael would be able to save for their dream house. So off she went home to sleep and tell Michael the news. She also phoned Matron's office to make an appointment to give in her notice. Then with a happy smile to herself Joan went off to bed. When Michael came home disgruntled about work, they were so busy but the union were making trouble with more strikes forecasted and lots of work. However, when Joan told him her good news, he cheered up and they had a happy weekend together. So that on Monday, Joan saw Matron and gave in her month's notice and was wished good luck by Matron and given a good reference to take away with her. Joan told the ward staff when she returned from her holiday. In the meantime, Kate had got a young English nurse from the night agency. Her name was Clare and Kate had to tell her all over again about the job as she had told Joan but not about the dismissed nurse. Clare took it all in and settled down to formalise herself with the equipment at her first night. She had found Kate a little difficult to always understand but she had done some industrial nursing in Dagenham in London before she came north to her husband's homeland. Her husband was from Glasgow. Once the night security and first aider had visited her. Clare settled down for her first patients. The night was fairly quiet, and Clare dutifully wrote all the names down with the surname, 'Do you Ken'. She did not notice this until Kate Appeared next morning. Kate roared with laughter and had to explain to Clare that 'Do you Ken' means, 'Do you know' (an Ayrshire expression). Clare laughed too and they got on well after this mix up.

In the meantime, Joan was working her notice and looking forward to her new job. Kate had told her she would order a uniform for her and advised her to see if there were a pair of toe-capped shoes around next time she came to the plant. Joan had to bring in her documents to the office for her to be put on the payroll. She was delighted when she was told her pay as it was twice what she had ever earned in all her days in the NHS. Now summer was coming and it was quite warm. One day when she came on nights, Kate met her with a grim face. Some of the men had walked out as they had been sitting in the sun at the lunch break and had then come to the medical room with headaches, thus wanting to go home! However, the management had said 'It was self-inflicted injury' and that they would not be paid for the afternoon shift. The union had objected and the whole shift had walked out. The management were correct as this was army regulations in hot weather. As it was so rarely hot in Glasgow and many men had pale or red skin it was a hazard for them. Luckily by nightfall, everything had calmed down and Joan was able to carry on with the men, all working hard. The car industry was busy just now and so the time past with some injuries requiring hospitalisation, others only mild treatment. Joan found that if it was a serious accident the men were very helpful.

One night, an agitated man arrived at the medical door saying, "Come quickly." A man up on a scaffolding was having a Seizure. Joan was lifted up in a basket to find the man foaming at the mouth. She quickly inserted a peg and then the man relaxed and the seizure was over. Joan with the first aider escorted the drowsy man down to the medical room to sleep the seizure off. It was the first time Joan had been up in a basket; quite an experience. Once the man recovered, Joan was able to establish that this was the man's first attack and he was frightened he would lose his job but Joan was able to reassure him that would not happen and sent him home. Joan told Kate all the details, and she would follow it all up. Kate told Joan that she might need her to help on day duty to do some home visits on long-term sickness. Kate said if Joan did one week as well as some admin work, Kate would see her pay was not affected and get Clair back for our nights. Joan was quite happy to oblige as it would give her some time to see her parents and other friends in the evenings. Some of the places the long-term sick-lived needed her to be taken there and back; so, her father was happy to drive her. Certain parts of Glasgow you cannot venture alone. Joan's father sat in the car whilst Joan climb up the dirty stairs to the dishevelled flats to see men lounging about but always with a long-term sick note. This was a real problem for the company because with sick notes, dismissal was not possible or the union would cause trouble. The other job, Joan was asked to do was check the time clocking. It had been recurred that there had been people clocking in for each other; as more than 15 minutes late was a pay cut. Joan found some discrepancies and gave them to Kate who would take them up with both the union and management.

After a week, Joan was quite happy to go back on her nights. One late summer night, Joan came to work to find the place empty. Kate was there to tell Joan a man had died on the plant that day and in respect to the widow everyone had walked out. It would have been better if the men had donated their wages for that day and night to the widow! So, life went on, and Joan and Kate had become good friends. In September Kate said she was going on holiday for two weeks, so would Joan do day duty and they would get Claire again for Nights. Joan was pleased to oblige and get to know the day shift more. Altogether, Joan was enjoying her new job but poor Michael was getting more and more disgruntled. He kept on thinking of his friends who had gone abroad.

Chapter 17

Joan was quite settled in her industrial night-duty job and happy to have each weekend off. Whilst Michael was getting more and more unsettled in the shipyards. There was continuous hassle and disputes; the work was running out. The future seemed bleak. The order books were empty and the men were all disgruntled. Michael again thought of his friends who had gone abroad. He decided to mention his idea to Joan. Perhaps they could go to Australia. There was a shipyard in Adelaide and surely a hospital for Joan. Buying a house in Glasgow with the uncertainty of his job would be difficult especially as the estate agents needed a good regular wage for a mortgage. So, one Friday night when Joan and Michael were sitting down after dinner, Michael turned to Joan with this idea, "Let's go to Australia." Joan was aghast. "Why?" she said. Michael Started to explain about what was happening at work. How he saw no future there and his worry about finding his own house as well. Joan looked at Michael's sad face. Giving him a big hug, she suggested that they would firstly look for a house. Then perhaps things might improve at the shipyards. So, they went off to bed with these ideas in their heads. Next morning, they started to visit the estate agents and looked at a few houses around their Area. They saw a nice four in the block in King's park near Joan's parents. They visited her parents for a coffee and discussed their plans. Joan's father said he would make some enquiries about small houses for them. Joan and Michael had the schedule for the four in the block house and were happy over the weekend to think about it and Joan said she could go and see the estate agent on Monday as she would not start work until Monday night.

On Monday morning, Joan took herself off to the estate agent. She saw a nice young man and they discussed all the details. However, there was a stumbling block. The mortgage people would not consider her wages although her job was more secure than Michael and better paid. Now they had a problem. Joan went home and rang her mother to ask her to come over for lunch. Joan's mother was delighted to have lunch with her daughter but was a little nervous about Joan's plans. Mum and daughter had a nice lunch and sat back in the living room to talk. Joan told her mum about the problem with the lovely house they liked and how happy she was at work but so worried about Michael being so unsettled Joan's mum suggested the four of them would have Sunday lunch together next weekend and discuss it all. Joan thought that was a great idea. So off Joan's mum went to talk to her husband and Joan awaited Michael heavy steps into the flat. His face was a picture of misery. Joan put the dinner on the table in silence and looked at Michael in sadness.

"Oh, what is coming next?" Joan had a good idea.

"Let's go and see the 'Humblebums'." Michael knew Billy Connolly as he was a welder in the shipyards and everyone said he was good. So Joan got tickets and they had a great night out to cheer Michael up.

Then Joan and Michael went to her parents for Sunday lunch and they all discussed Joan and Michael's problem. Joan's father offered to help them look for a house and give them the deposit but that did not sit well with Michael. When they got home, Michael said to Joan that he was going to write to his friend in Adelaide. Joan remembered a girl who went from the 'Royal' to Australia. Michael sat down to write to his friend Joe. He wrote to the shipyard as he had no address for Joe. So, Michael and Joan continued to look for a house viewing a few but the enthusiasm had gone out of the idea for them both. Joan's mum phoned on Monday morning asking Joan to come over whilst Michael was working. Joan's mum sensed something was going on with them. Joan went over Monday afternoon after a leisurely morning as she was on duty that night. Joan's mum made tea and then Joan told her mother about Michael's idea. Joan's mum was naturally upset but understood where Michael was coming from. Her mum said she would speak to her husband about Australia. Joan's mum was a sensible person and realised Michael was unhappy and this makes an unhappy household. Perhaps they should let them go to Australia. It was not such a bad idea and that she and dad could come and visit as they were still fit and able. Joan was a little scared of leaving them but was so worried about Michael and the lack of security at the shipyard. It would all be a new beginning and she would surely find a nursing job there. She remembered one of the girls in her course going off to Australia on the £10 trip. You had to stay three years, she remembered. However, she could not remember the girl's name. She would phone her friends at the 'Royal' perhaps someone would remember the girl.

So off Joan went home and make dinner before going into work. Michael came home in a better mood and was still happy to go on looking for a house in Glasgow whilst he contacted his friend, Joe. Joan went into work but said nothing to Kate. When Joan contacted a friend at the 'Royal', the friend remembered the girl who went to Australia and said she would look out the name and address of this girl. This friend of Joan's from the 'Royal' phoned mid-week with the news that the girl who went to Australia and was still there is in Adelaide. Her name and address were: Jennifer % Flinders hospital there. So, Joan wrote off a letter to her. Now both Joan and Michael would have to wait for replies from their letters. In the meantime, they would just have to be patient and keep looking out for a house here at home. Michael finished work at lunchtime on Friday and asked Joan to meet him in town to go to the recruiting agency for Australia. So, they could find out all the details about the £10 trip out there. They got a nice girl with all the knowledge about Adelaide. She told them the shipyard was doing well and there was a beautiful hospital there with a high reputation as a training hospital. So, Joan and Michael asked what they needed to do next. They were told to hand in a CV including payslips for the last year. Then the authorities would firstly consider their financial situation regarding the £10 trip. Also, they would await replies from their letters to their friends in Adelaide. Michael and Joan went away quite excited. The trip would be by boat and take three weeks. A real holiday for them. However, they were told not to say anything at their work meantime. Letters were needed to arrive and finances to be sorted.

Chapter 18

Joan and Michael continued to work away not saying anything to their workmates. They continued to look at houses but were rebuffed each time regarding a mortgage as no one would take into consideration, Joan's good wages. Michael was really fed up and kept waiting for news from Australia. However, patience was the thing and at last two letters on the same day came for each of them. Michael's was from the shipyard with not only a nice letter but an offer of a job too. Joan's was a chatty letter telling her that Flinders hospital was always looking for British nurses. So now they decided to approach the Agency dealing with recruitment for Australia. They went on the Friday afternoon after Michael finished work and Joan had had a rest. The gentleman they saw was an Australian himself from Sydney. He was very helpful and explained all the necessary requirements but said it would not be difficult for either of them as they both had offers of work. Accommodation would be no problem. So, the process could go ahead. Both Michael and Joan were getting excited. They decided to go and see Joan's parents and tell them their plans.

Joan's father was delighted for them. Her mother a little nervous of saying farewell to her only daughter but they both realised that it was their future. Joan told her parents that once they would be settled, they should come out. Her parents were young enough to be able to travel and being retired would choose when to travel. However, it would take a while and both Joan and Michael had to have special medicals, financial interviews as they were going on the £10 experience. The ship would sail from Tilbury in London. Joan's parents would travel to London with them. Now the wait started but there were no real problems; no house to sell only notices to be given at their works. Joan's mum decided to give them a going away party and Joan invited her friends from the 'Royal' as well as Kate who was sad to lose Joan. Michael invited a few of his friends from work.

The party was in Joan's parents' house with a lovely buffet. Many people brought going away presents, and Joan and Michael were quite overwhelmed. Joan and her mother went into town one day to buy some more summer clothes as it looked like it would be early spring when they would leave Scotland and as it would take three weeks to get there; Joan would not need all her winter clothes. So, Joan's mother took her into town to buy an evening dress as well as summer clothes. Michael refused to buy a kilt as he had hired one for the wedding. So, he brought a dinner suit for the captain's dinner. They were all ready, so Joan, Michael and her parents set off for Tilbury, London. They had a great send off at central station from all their friends. In London, Joan's father had arranged a good hotel and a real British dinner with lentil soup and smoked salmon followed by steak pie and all the trimmings and chicken pie. Needless to say, it was all followed by Ice-cream and apple pie or custard. Next morning, they were all up early and took off to Tilbury.

The ship stood proudly waiting at the dockside and clutching their tickets, Joan and Michael boarded their home for the next 25 days. Waving goodbye tearfully, Joan's parents stood on the shore as the ship sailed away. Now Joan and Michael had a holiday to look forward to before their new adventure. Their cabin had an air conditioner, a radio and a sweet little bathroom with a shower. The steward knocked on the door to introduce himself. His name was Alan and he told them he would pull their bunks down each night and put them away in the morning. The swimming pool attracted Joan as well as the walk around the deck. Michael was interested in the layout of the ship and got himself an invitation to the bridge. He feared he would get bored on the long journey but at the captain's dinner the captain spoke to him and realised he was a shipyard worker and arranged for him to meet the crew and go below deck. Michael was very pleased. In the meantime, Joan had found other couples who were emigrating like themselves. Some were going to other towns but she found one couple going to Adelaide. The couple had been on a cruise before and told Joan there was a sickbay with a full medical staff as they might be needed when they went through the Bay of Biscay. Joan took herself off to meet the medical staff. However, Joan and Michael appeared to be good sailors and did not need any medical help but some of the other passengers did.

One day, the captain called a meeting for all the people emigrating and divided them into the various towns they were going too. Ladies from each town spoke to them. Michael and Joan asked about accommodation and were assured they would have good places to stay near to their work. A lady called Lily told them just to follow her when they would land and not to worry. Lily was even able to show them a photo of their new home. Joan sat down on the sundeck to write to her parents with all the news. Sydney was their arrival point and a train would take them, Lily and the other couple on to Adelaide. It was all so exciting for Michael and Joan. A new life, a new home and new jobs. It made them happy but nervous. So, the ship would soon arrive in Sydney – a new beginning.